THERE'S A NIGHTMARE
IN MY CLOSET

written and illustrated by Mercer Mayer

Dial Books for Young Readers
New York

Copyright © 1968 by Mercer Mayer • All rights reserved
Library of Congress catalog card number: 68-15250 • First Pied Piper printing 1976
A Pied Piper Book is a registered trademark of Dial Books for Young Readers
A division of NAL Penguin Inc.
® TM 1,163,686 and ® TM 1,054,312
Printed in the United States of America • C O B E • 20
THERE'S A NIGHTMARE IN MY CLOSET is published in a hardcover edition by
Dial Books for Young Readers • 2 Park Avenue • New York, New York 10016

10 9 8 7 6 5 4 3

Marianna

From cotton to rabbit

There used to be a nightmare in my closet.

Before going to sleep,

I always closed the closet door.

I was even afraid to turn around and look.

When I was safe in bed, I'd peek...

sometimes.

One night I decided to get rid of my nightmare
once and for all.

As soon as the room was dark, I heard
him creeping toward me.

Quickly I turned on the light and caught him
sitting at the foot of my bed.

"Go away, Nightmare, or I'll shoot you," I said.

I shot him anyway.

My nightmare began to cry.

I was mad...

but not too mad.

"Nightmare, be quiet or you'll wake
Mommy and Daddy," I said.

He wouldn't stop crying so I took
him by the hand

and tucked him in bed

and closed the closet door.

I suppose there's another nightmare in my
closet, but my bed's not big enough for three.